Woman of the Hour

The Untold Crimes and Deceptions of Rodney Alcala

Oliver patrick

Copyright

All rights reserved. No part of this book may be reproduced, stored in a retrieval system, or transmitted in any form or by any means, electronic, mechanical, photocopying, recording, or otherwise, without the prior written permission of the publisher, except for brief quotations used in reviews.

This book is a work of nonfiction. Any similarity to real persons, living or dead, is coincidental and not intended by the author.

© **2024 by Oliver patrick**

Disclaimer

Woman of the Hour: The Untold Crimes and Deceptions of Rodney Alcala contains detailed accounts of true events, including descriptions of violent crimes, psychological manipulation, and disturbing subject matter. This book aims to provide an accurate, respectful portrayal of Rodney Alcala's life and crimes, drawing from court records, media reports, and extensive research.

While every effort has been made to handle sensitive information with care, reader discretion is strongly advised. This book is intended for mature audiences and serves to raise awareness about the consequences of unchecked deception and violence, as well as to honor the memory of Alcala's victims.

Table of Contents

Introduction..6
   Chapter One..11
   The Notorious Contestant..................................11
   The Concealed Predator.....................................19
Chapter Three...26
   The Real Victims...26
   The Hunt for a Killer..33
   The Dating Game Killer....................................40
Chapter Six..46
   The Film Adaptation..46
Chapter Seven...54
   The Killer's Legacy...54
Chapter Eight...63
   The Convergence of Media and Violence...............63

Introduction

On September 13, 1978, millions of television viewers tuned in for an episode of The Dating Game, a lighthearted show where single men and women navigated playful, flirtatious questions in hopes of winning a date. That night's episode featured a seemingly charming and handsome bachelor named Rodney Alcala, who presented himself as a suave photographer. His charisma won over bachelorette Cheryl Bradshaw, who ultimately chose him as her date. But beneath his charming facade lurked a dark secret—Rodney Alcala was in the middle of a killing spree, his hands already stained with the blood of multiple victims. The viewers, audience members, and even the producers of the show had no inkling that they were watching a cold-blooded serial killer who would soon claim even more lives.

This isn't just a tale of a game show going wrong; it's the haunting story of a predator who cloaked himself in charisma, intelligence, and charm to evade justice. Woman of the Hour: The True Story of Rodney Alcala and His Horrifying Crimes unpacks one of America's most disturbing cases of serial murder, unraveling how Alcala managed to lead a double life: one as a seemingly benign participant in the world of entertainment, the other as a calculated, merciless killer.

At the core of this story lies the unsettling intersection of media, allure, and violence. How did Rodney Alcala—a convicted felon with a sinister past—manage to step onto the stage of a prime-time show and captivate an audience? What does his story reveal about the power and responsibility of media in shaping public perception, and how easily viewers can be misled by a well-curated image? This book probes these pressing questions, delving into the disturbing reality of Alcala's crimes and the larger societal implications they expose.

Beyond the chilling media spectacle, however, lie the lives of his victims—women and young girls who were senselessly taken from the world. This book seeks to honor their memories by shedding light on their lives, their loved ones, and the families left to grapple with unimaginable loss.

Through exhaustive research, meticulous examination of court documents, media reports, and interviews, Woman of the Hour reconstructs Alcala's life and reveals the relentless efforts of law enforcement to stop him. It's a story of unyielding evil, but also of the resilience of those who fought tirelessly to bring him to justice.

As you delve into this book, prepare to confront unsettling truths about Alcala's life and crimes, and the disconcerting reality of how he deceived so many for so long. This haunting tale stands as a stark reminder of the dangers hiding behind ordinary facades and how the allure of media can obscure the darker truths beneath.

Chapter One

The Notorious Contestant

Rodney Alcala wasn't just another face on *The Dating Game*. In 1978, as millions of viewers watched the lighthearted show, Alcala's charming smile and confident responses made him seem like any other contestant hoping to win a date. His flirtatious quips and smooth delivery painted him as an ideal suitor. But behind the camera-ready facade was a man whose darkness ran terrifyingly deep. Rodney Alcala had already begun a spree of heinous crimes, leaving a trail of innocent lives destroyed. Unbeknownst to the audience, Alcala was a predator hiding behind a mask of charm.

As he bantered with bachelorette Cheryl Bradshaw, Alcala's flirtatious line, "I'm called the banana, and I look really good… peel me," drew laughter from the crowd. To them, he was just another charismatic bachelor, but underneath that wit was a violent man whose sinister intentions remained hidden. Cheryl chose him as her date, yet when it came time to meet him offstage, she sensed something unsettling about Alcala. Recalling the encounter years later, she admitted, "He was creepy. Something just didn't feel right." Trusting her instincts, she ultimately canceled the date—a choice that may have saved her life.

This bizarre intersection of entertainment and horror brings us face to face with the chilling truth that a serial killer once stood confidently on national television, charming an unwitting audience. Alcala's presence on *The Dating Game* is a stark reminder of the deceptive power of charm. Despite a past littered with violent crimes, Alcala managed to elude capture and continue his dark path. Born in 1943, he grew up intelligent, well-educated, and outwardly artistic, even studying at the New York University

School of Fine Arts. But his interest in photography soon became his tool for luring victims.

In 1968, he assaulted eight-year-old Tali Shapiro in his apartment. Although a witness called the police, and they arrived just in time to save Tali, Alcala fled before he could be arrested. Using the alias John Berger, he lived on the East Coast, avoiding detection for years and pursuing his photography. Underneath his normal life, however, Alcala continued to nurture his violent tendencies. His crimes grew in number and brutality over the next decade, each one meticulously concealed behind his veneer of charisma. By the time he appeared on *The*

Dating Game, Alcala was already a serial killer, responsible for the deaths of numerous young women.

Even under investigation for the murder of twelve-year-old Robin Samsoe, Alcala confidently auditioned for the show, knowing his charm could disguise the predator within. The producers, unaware of his criminal past, saw only his alluring personality and accepted him as a contestant. Back then, background checks were minimal, and Alcala's good looks and witty responses fit the show's playful tone. For the audience, his flirtation was entertaining, but it was horrifyingly deceptive—just months earlier, Alcala had lured Samsoe into his web of cruelty.

She was simply riding her bike to ballet class when she vanished. Her remains were found days later, but without solid evidence, Alcala was still free to charm the nation.

His appearance on *The Dating Game* has since become almost surreal to watch. His wide smile, casual confidence, and joking responses all take on a sinister weight knowing the horrific crimes he'd committed. In the months following the show, Alcala was arrested for Samsoe's murder, and as investigators delved into his past, they discovered even more victims. His case shocked the country, revealing the deadly consequences of a charming predator lurking in plain sight. Over time, Alcala would be tried and convicted for multiple murders, his true count of victims likely far higher than anyone initially realized.

The horror of Rodney Alcala's story is twofold—not just in the lives he took, but in how successfully he hid among us. Again and again, he managed to slip through the justice system, leveraging his intelligence and charm to manipulate those around him. Alcala's stint on *The Dating Game* was perhaps the most chilling example of this manipulation, a performance for a national audience that masked the monstrous reality beneath. Today, his appearance on the show remains a haunting symbol of how deeply deceptive charm can be, a reminder that predators often wear the friendliest faces.

Since his conviction, Alcala's story has fascinated and horrified the public, sparking countless books, documentaries, and podcasts. Each retelling forces us to confront the eerie truth about how a man so dangerous went undetected for so long. *Woman of the Hour* brings this dark tale back into the light, forcing us to recognize how easily we can be deceived. Cheryl Bradshaw's intuition may have seemed trivial at the time, but it likely saved her life. Her decision not to follow through with the date serves as a sobering reminder of the importance of trusting our instincts. In a world where danger often hides behind the most ordinary of faces, her story remains a testament to the power of intuition and the haunting truth that even monsters can smile.

Chapter Two

The Concealed Predator

Rodney Alcala, infamously dubbed the "Dating Game Killer," was a man who embodied charm and intellect, a combination that he wielded as weapons. With an artist's eye, a smooth voice, and a sophisticated air, he easily disarmed those around him, hiding his true nature behind a mask of civility. But beneath this beguiling facade lay something horrifying—Rodney Alcala was a predator, a master of deception who lured, trapped, and ultimately destroyed his victims with chilling precision. His horrific acts shocked the nation, leaving a haunting imprint on the annals of crime that would captivate investigators and the media for decades.

Alcala's dark journey didn't begin with his appearance on *The Dating Game*; it took root long before, set against a backdrop of early trauma and inner darkness. Born in San Antonio, Texas, in 1943, Alcala's childhood was marked by abandonment when his father left, prompting a move to Los Angeles. Despite his troubled start, he excelled academically, showing an artistic flair and intelligence that seemed to promise a bright future. Yet, even as a young man, subtle signs hinted at the darkness within. His inner turmoil would soon manifest in ways no one could have anticipated.

After high school, Alcala joined the U.S. Army, where he suffered a mental breakdown, going AWOL before receiving a diagnosis of antisocial personality disorder. This diagnosis, though a stark warning of his capacity for harm, did little to hinder his reintegration into society. He went on to study at UCLA, sharpening his skills as a manipulator while concealing a growing need for power and control. His charm allowed him to slip unnoticed into the lives of others, a predator in plain sight.

In 1968, Alcala's first known assault sent shockwaves through the community. He lured eight-year-old Tali Shapiro into his car under the pretense of giving her a ride to school, only to take her to his apartment and brutally assault her. A concerned witness tipped off the police, saving Tali's life just in time. But by the time authorities arrived, Alcala had already fled, setting off on a years-long spree that saw him assuming aliases and concealing his monstrous nature under layers of charm.

Reinventing himself as "John Berger" in New York City, Alcala pursued film studies at New York University, where he studied under Roman Polanski. His camera became both a tool of his craft and a lure for his victims, a means of disarming young women and girls. He offered them the promise of professional photos, convincing them to lower their guard. But once they were alone, Alcala revealed his true nature, employing a methodical brutality that became his dark signature.

His cunning and ability to lead a double life allowed him to evade capture for years, even landing him a spot on the FBI's Ten Most Wanted list. In a twist of fate, he was ultimately recognized by two children from a wanted poster, leading to his arrest and extradition to California. Despite being charged in Tali Shapiro's attack, he manipulated the legal system, striking a plea deal and serving only a brief sentence. In less than three years, Alcala was back on the streets, free to continue his spree.

Following his release, Alcala resumed his killing with renewed intensity. Among his victims was twelve-year-old Robin Samsoe, whose tragic disappearance and subsequent murder stunned the community. Her remains were discovered in the rugged hills of the San Gabriel Mountains, sparking a hunt that ultimately led police back to Alcala. Inside his home, investigators found over

1,000 photographs of women and children—haunting mementos, many of whom remain unidentified. These images are believed to be the remnants of countless lives destroyed by Alcala's hand.

His eventual conviction in Samsoe's murder set off a grueling series of trials that spanned decades, with convictions overturned on technicalities and procedural errors. In 2010, DNA evidence finally linked him to additional murders, solidifying his fate. As his own defense attorney, Alcala even presented the infamous *Dating Game* footage, displaying the chilling nonchalance that had concealed his depravity. In the footage, he charmed both the audience and bachelorette Cheryl Bradshaw, who selected him as her date. But Bradshaw sensed something wrong, and her refusal to meet him again likely saved her life. This televised moment became a disturbing reminder of how effortlessly predators like Alcala can hide in plain sight.

Rodney Alcala's story isn't merely a recounting of his horrific crimes; it's a grim reflection on the power of charm as a disguise for evil. Alcala's final conviction in 2010 closed a harrowing chapter in American crime history, but the true scope of his crimes may never be known. Some believe his victims number over 130, an estimate based in part on the countless haunting photos he left behind.

Until his death in prison in 2021, Alcala remained devoid of remorse, taking with him secrets of unimaginable cruelty. His life, crimes, and the chilling ease with which he concealed his true nature serve as an enduring reminder:

sometimes, the greatest evil hides behind the most disarming smiles.

Chapter Three

The Real Victims

Rodney Alcala, the "Dating Game Killer," wasn't merely a predator hiding behind charm and sophistication; he left countless lives devastated in his wake. While *Woman of the Hour* dives into the shocking story of his crimes, it's essential to look beyond the sensationalism and remember the real people forever impacted by his cruelty. Alcala's victims were not merely faces or names in a tragic story—they were daughters, sisters, friends, and young women filled with hopes, dreams, and bright futures stolen from them by a man who pretended to be trustworthy, only to unleash unspeakable violence.

Each of Alcala's victims represents the terrible human cost of his unchecked evil. These were not random targets but women and girls he lured with promises of photography or artistic mentorship, exploiting their trust for his own twisted desires. Most were young and full of life, caught in a predator's snare simply because they believed in the kindness he projected.

Robin Samsoe, one of Alcala's youngest victims, was a 12-year-old girl who disappeared on her way to ballet class in Huntington Beach, California, in 1979. She was an energetic, lively child with her whole life ahead of her. When her remains were found days later, her tragic loss shattered her community and ignited the investigation that eventually led to Alcala's arrest. Robin's death struck a chord across the nation, as her innocence underscored the depth of Alcala's cruelty.

But Robin was not the first nor the last. Among Alcala's early known victims was Cornelia Crilley, a 23-year-old flight attendant living in New York City, found strangled in her apartment in 1971. She had dreams of adventure and a promising career, only to be taken in by Alcala's deceptive charm. It would take decades for investigators to link Alcala to her murder, as the technology to bring justice lagged behind his crimes.

Jill Barcomb, an 18-year-old runaway hoping for a fresh start in Los Angeles, was another victim. She had escaped a difficult life in New York only to cross paths with Alcala, who cruelly ended her life and discarded her body in the Hollywood Hills in 1977. Jill's dreams of renewal were cut short, her life stolen just as she was beginning to carve out her path.

Then there was Georgia Wixted, a 27-year-old nurse, known for her compassion and dedication to helping others. In 1977, she was brutally murdered in her apartment after Alcala lured her in with promises of professional photography. Her friends and family remembered her as a selfless, kind-hearted person who committed her life to saving others, only to have her own life taken by a man who preyed on her goodwill.

Charlotte Lamb, a 32-year-old legal secretary, crossed paths with Alcala in 1978. After a long day at work, she encountered the man who would end her life, leaving her body cruelly posed in a laundry room. And Jill Parenteau, a 21-year-old with a friendly spirit and love for life, was just starting out, working as a keypunch operator in Burbank, when she met Alcala. Her friends remember her smile and joy for life—a light extinguished far too soon.

What Alcala did was not merely murder; it was a calculated, sadistic pattern designed to strip his victims of both dignity and life. For years, he evaded capture, capitalizing on the era's limited forensic methods and his own manipulative charm. As he moved between New York and California, blending into new communities under various aliases, Alcala left a trail of shattered families and dreams behind him, his charm masking an unimaginable darkness.

The grief experienced by the families of these women is profound, a pain intensified by the knowledge of the horrors their loved ones endured. Robin Samsoe's mother, Marianne Connelly, fought tirelessly for justice, becoming an outspoken advocate for victims' rights. Her strength in the face of tragedy is a testament to the resilience of those left to pick up the pieces, as they live with the haunting knowledge that their loved ones' last moments were filled with terror.

When we remember Rodney Alcala's story, we should focus not on the twisted allure of a killer who hid behind a charming facade, but on the lives he destroyed. Each of his victims was more than a part of his crime spree; they were individuals with unique dreams, ambitions, and loved ones who mourn them still. As we reflect on this dark chapter, let us honor them not for how they died, but for the lives they lived—lives that were full, bright, and ended far too soon.

Chapter Four

The Hunt for a Killer

Rodney Alcala's crimes spanned decades, leaving a harrowing trail of broken lives and lingering grief. Behind a facade of charm and sophistication, Alcala hid his true self—a cunning predator with a calculating mind, who used his intellect and charisma to lure unsuspecting victims into his twisted web. For years, he lived among society undetected, blending in as just another face in the crowd. Yet behind his friendly smile was a man capable of unfathomable brutality, his heinous acts concealed by a veneer of charm.

Alcala's ability to evade capture for so long speaks to his skill at deception and the gaps in the justice system of the time. He traveled across states, leaving a trail of victims from California to New York, exploiting a fragmented law enforcement system that lacked the coordination to connect his crimes. It wasn't until the tragic disappearance of 12-year-old Robin Samsoe in the summer of 1979 that the authorities focused on him as a prime suspect. Robin, a bright and joyful young girl, had been heading to ballet class when she encountered Alcala. Her remains, found 12 days later in a remote area of the Sierra Madre Mountains, marked a turning point in the investigation. Her community's devastation and search for justice ignited the hunt that would finally bring Alcala to light.

Alcala's charm initially shielded him from suspicion; even those close to him couldn't fathom the horrors he concealed. He often posed as a professional photographer, promising young women and children opportunities that he would never fulfill. Once he earned their trust, he turned violent, ruthlessly ending their lives and leaving them as though they were nothing more than discarded objects. His meticulous approach and transient lifestyle allowed him to evade suspicion, moving between communities and adopting aliases that helped him hide in plain sight.

When authorities searched Alcala's apartment, they uncovered a cache of photographs—hundreds of young women and children, captured in vulnerable and compromising positions. Some had believed they were modeling, others were simply caught unguarded. For many of these women, their photographs became haunting reminders of their tragic fates. Investigators soon realized that these images could hold the key to solving more unsolved cases. As they tried to match faces with missing persons and cold cases, they unearthed even more victims—lives he had stolen, families left shattered without answers.

One of the most chilling aspects of Alcala's trial was his audacity. He represented himself, manipulating the courtroom as he had manipulated his victims. His arrogance was palpable, and the media coverage surrounding the trial highlighted the disturbingly composed demeanor of a man who had committed such horrifying acts. As details of his crimes came to light, the public was horrified by the extent of his cruelty: he didn't just kill—he inflicted suffering, relishing the control he held over his victims' final moments.

In 2003, advancements in DNA technology connected Alcala to additional murders from the 1970s, revealing a pattern that stretched across both coasts and over years. The evidence was damning, but for the families of his victims, each new revelation brought a fresh wave of grief and anger. Alcala's case, which spanned multiple trials and appeals, exposed significant failures in the justice system—a system that allowed him to avoid accountability for so long, granting him the freedom to continue his spree.

For many families, the pain of their loss endures, intensified by the realization that Alcala's victims may number far beyond those identified.

The photographs found in his possession remain a chilling testament to the unknown lives he impacted. Even in the face of conviction, some families are left without closure, their loved ones' faces frozen in images that tell a story too horrible to contemplate.

Rodney Alcala's story is more than the tale of a serial killer—it is a profound lesson on the dangers of surface-level perceptions and the importance of vigilance. He was the man no one suspected, the friendly photographer, the charming suitor, and the contestant on *The Dating Game* who won over an audience with ease. But beneath that smile was a mind filled with violence, a predator exploiting his charm to mask his true nature. Alcala's legacy is one of unimaginable horror, a reminder of the enduring scars left by those who prey on the vulnerable.

The story, as told in *Woman of the Hour*, captures not only Alcala's cruelty but also the resilience of the families who have fought for decades to keep the memory of their loved ones alive and to seek justice for those who suffered in silence.

Chapter Five

The Dating Game Killer

Rodney Alcala's story is one of the most chilling tales of a serial killer who, for years, managed to evade capture while charming his way into the lives of his unsuspecting victims and the public eye. His case is uniquely disturbing because he used a national television appearance, on *The Dating Game,* as a stage to mask his dark nature, presenting himself to millions as a charismatic bachelor. Behind the smile and playful wit was a man who had already committed unspeakable crimes, a predator hiding in plain sight, driven by a twisted mind that would lead him to commit some of the most brutal murders in American history.

Alcala's appearance on *The Dating Game* wasn't merely an eerie moment in his criminal life—it was a calculated move to maintain his carefully constructed facade. By 1978, he had already taken the lives of several women, yet there he stood, confidently assuming the role of Bachelor Number One, laughing and flirting with the bachelorette, Cheryl Bradshaw. His performance was so convincing that Bradshaw chose him as her date. Fortunately, she trusted her instincts, later declining the date, describing him as "creepy." That instinct may have saved her life.

Alcala's ability to charm his way onto the show highlights one of the darkest aspects of his story: the ease with which he manipulated not only those around him but also a national audience. His good looks and smooth demeanor allowed him to blend into society, using his charisma as a weapon to disarm others. He posed as a professional photographer, offering opportunities to young women that never existed, gaining their trust only to betray it in the most horrific ways. For Alcala, his time on *The Dating Game* wasn't about finding romance but about maintaining the mask that concealed his true intentions.

By the time of his television appearance, Alcala was a seasoned killer. The ease with which he won over the crowd reflected his ability to compartmentalize his life—on one side, a charming, witty bachelor; on the other, a sadistic predator. His victims were often young women and girls who he lured into isolated areas under the guise of photography, a manipulation that allowed him to reveal his true nature only once they were alone. His crimes were not only about control but about inflicting the maximum amount of pain, a sadistic pattern that left lasting scars on the lives of those he touched.

Alcala's crimes went undetected for years, not only because of his cunning but also because of systemic failures. Despite multiple arrests for violent offenses, he managed to slip through the cracks of a justice system that failed to recognize the true extent of his menace. His capture in 1979, following the murder of 12-year-old Robin Samsoe, marked a breakthrough, but the legal process was marred by repeated delays, retrials, and appeals. Each appeal reopened old wounds for the families of his victims, who watched him evade full accountability even as more evidence connected him to other unsolved murders.

In 2010, decades after his appearance on *The Dating Game*, Alcala was sentenced to death for the murders of five women. Still, investigators believe his victim count could be as high as 130. His crimes serve as a haunting reminder of how easily evil can hide behind a friendly face, and his story exposed serious flaws in the justice system and the entertainment industry's vetting processes.

For the families of Alcala's victims, his time on *The Dating Game* is a reminder of his chilling double life, of how he could enjoy the spotlight while leaving them in the dark about the fate of their loved ones. Alcala wasn't just a killer; he was a sadist who inflicted suffering with a level of brutality that shocked even the most experienced investigators. His story doesn't offer simple answers but rather a haunting glimpse into the disturbing truth that killers like Alcala can hide among us, blending in seamlessly, and, for a time, fooling everyone.

Chapter Six

The Film Adaptation

In 2023, *Woman of the Hour* premiered, pulling audiences into the haunting story of Rodney Alcala, one of America's most infamous serial killers. The film brings to life a man who charmed his way onto a national game show, concealing the horrors he had already committed and would continue to commit. By blending fact and fiction, the movie exposes the unsettling truth of how evil can hide in plain sight, weaving through daily life undetected. But beyond the chilling cinematography lies a reality darker than any fictional retelling—a narrative of Alcala's crimes that extends far beyond what the screen can convey.

Opening in the familiar, carefree setting of *The Dating Game*, the film shows Alcala as Bachelor Number One, smiling and effortlessly charming the bachelorette, Cheryl Bradshaw. Yet from the beginning, there's an undercurrent of tension. With a knowing nod to the audience's awareness of Alcala's crimes, the filmmakers avoid ambiguity, casting an ominous shadow over each of his charming responses. This juxtaposition of Alcala's public persona with his private monstrosities creates an experience of constant discomfort, amplifying the horror as viewers watch him shift between a charismatic contestant and a predator.

The film deftly navigates the contrast between Alcala's game show persona and his hidden life. One moment he's delivering flirty lines on camera, and in the next, we see him stalking his victims, using charm as a weapon. This duality is woven throughout the film, showing how effortlessly Alcala moved between his public and private worlds. His calculated manipulation of these two faces is as terrifying as his crimes, underscoring how easy it was for him to evade suspicion.

Woman of the Hour also honors Alcala's victims, particularly the women and young girls who crossed paths with him. Cheryl Bradshaw's character is central, representing the unknowingly close brush she had with a killer. Through flashbacks and careful pacing, the film brings depth to the victims, presenting them not merely as statistics but as individuals with dreams and loved ones. Each victim's portrayal is a powerful reminder of the lives they lived before they encountered Alcala's dark intentions.

Rather than resorting to graphic violence, the film emphasizes the trauma Alcala inflicted, grounding the horror in realism. Each violent scene is restrained yet harrowing, depicting not just the physical pain but also the psychological devastation he left behind. This realistic approach amplifies the horror, making clear that each crime had far-reaching impacts that devastated families, friends, and communities.

What makes *Woman of the Hour* especially effective is its nuanced portrayal of Alcala himself. Unlike the typical Hollywood depiction of serial killers as overtly menacing, Alcala is portrayed as an everyday man—charming, intelligent, and seemingly ordinary. He's shown as someone who could easily pass as a friendly stranger or a familiar face, a choice that adds layers to the horror by confronting viewers with the unsettling possibility that true danger often looks unremarkable.

Casting a relatively unknown actor as Alcala enhances this effect, allowing the audience to see him as an ordinary man capable of extraordinary evil. The actor's restrained performance captures Alcala's quiet menace, conveying a man who could smile warmly one moment and commit unthinkable violence the next. This portrayal shatters the mold of what viewers might expect a serial killer to look or act like, emphasizing how Alcala's innocuous appearance enabled him to hide in plain sight.

The film's pacing complements this portrayal, focusing not just on physical danger but on the psychological tension of Alcala's double life. Even his most polite conversations are fraught with dread, laden with the weight of what he conceals. As viewers, we're made to feel the same unease that his victims likely felt—a tension that builds with each scene, turning even his seemingly benign interactions into moments charged with fear.

However, while *Woman of the Hour* stays largely true to the facts, certain creative liberties were taken. Timelines are condensed, and some investigative details simplified, allowing the story to flow more naturally on screen. For instance, the film's portrayal of Alcala's capture is streamlined, leaving out the years of painstaking investigation that ultimately brought him to justice. Though these changes are understandable, they do blend history with fiction, creating a narrative that feels cohesive but is not wholly accurate.

Nonetheless, *Woman of the Hour* succeeds in its primary goal: exposing the chilling reality of a killer hiding in plain sight, evading capture for years. The film's commentary on fame and the dark side of public personas resonates deeply. Alcala's appearance on *The Dating Game* is a metaphor for how easily charm can deceive us, a warning that the face of evil often looks disturbingly normal. It's a haunting reminder of how those who seem safe and familiar can sometimes hide the darkest secrets.

In its final scenes, the film doesn't offer tidy resolutions or easy answers. Instead, it lingers on the lives destroyed, the families left grieving, and the scars Alcala's crimes left on countless lives. This discomfort is the film's greatest achievement, forcing us to confront the reality that sometimes, evil hides right before our eyes, masquerading as just another face in the crowd.

Chapter Seven

The Killer's Legacy

Rodney Alcala's story is one that sends a deep chill through anyone who encounters it—a dark tale of manipulation, charm, and shocking violence. Known as *The Dating Game Killer*, Alcala's crimes went beyond the brutality of his actions, extending into the sinister ease with which he slipped into society, even charming millions of viewers on national television. His legacy remains a horrifying testament to the lives he destroyed, the anguish he inflicted on countless families, and the haunting revelation of how he concealed his monstrous nature for years.

Alcala's ability to live a double life—as an ordinary man by day and a ruthless predator by night—continues to confound and terrify. His crimes spanned years, and for the families of his victims, justice came only after agonizing delays, repeated trials, and a series of devastating revelations. Long after his imprisonment, new evidence and advancing technology continued to uncover additional victims, some of whom had been lost to the shadows for decades.

To many, it seems incomprehensible that someone like Rodney Alcala could live undetected among them, hiding his violent acts behind an educated facade and a charming smile. His infamous appearance on *The Dating Game* in 1978 added a chilling layer to his story; on screen, he was a confident bachelor, selected by the bachelorette. But behind that calm demeanor lay the horrifying truth that he was already responsible for several murders. Alcala's charm and intelligence weren't just tools to win trust—they were keys to his long-standing evasion of justice. With every interaction, he left behind families haunted by unanswered questions and loved ones taken far too soon.

For the families of Alcala's victims, his legacy isn't a historical anecdote but an unending nightmare. The trauma and grief he caused are impossible to quantify. Many families endured years of uncertainty, with no closure or answers as they searched for lost daughters, sisters, and mothers. And for those who finally learned of his involvement in their loved ones' deaths, the truth brought bittersweet relief tempered with a renewed pain. For these families, Rodney Alcala wasn't a character from a distant true-crime story—he was the real source of their loss and enduring sorrow.

Alcala's trial gripped the public, yet the evidence presented was often too disturbing for many to stomach. Despite overwhelming proof of his guilt, Alcala continued to deny responsibility, even when DNA evidence linked him to multiple murders. His refusal to acknowledge his crimes deprived his victims' families of the full closure they desperately sought, leaving them in a purgatory of unresolved pain.

Even in prison, Alcala remained a manipulative force. Representing himself in court, he displayed an arrogance that was both chilling and infuriating to the families of his victims. His courtroom demeanor was a stark reminder of the calculated cruelty he wielded, seemingly reveling in the control he still held over the proceedings. For those who had already suffered from his crimes, watching him claim the spotlight once more was a bitter reminder of the torment he had inflicted.

Justice was a slow and painful process in Alcala's case. Initially sentenced to death in 1980 for the murder of 12-year-old Robin Samsoe, his conviction was overturned twice on procedural grounds, forcing victims' families to relive the trauma of the trials. With each retrial, they faced fresh waves of anguish as Alcala continued to prolong the process, reasserting his control over the system and forcing his victims' loved ones to endure his presence once more.

It wasn't until 2010, after decades of legal battles, that Alcala was finally convicted for five murders, linked through DNA evidence to the deaths of Robin Samsoe, Georgia Wixted, Jill Barcomb, Charlotte Lamb, and Jill Parenteau. Investigators believe, however, that his true number of victims could be far higher. With each new piece of evidence, the scope of his crimes widened, raising disturbing questions about how many more lives he may have taken. His final victim count remains unknown, but some estimates suggest he may have killed dozens more.

Even after Alcala's final conviction, the full extent of his crimes continued to surface. Investigators discovered a cache of photographs depicting numerous young women and children, some of whom were later identified as his victims, while many others remain unknown. These photographs are haunting reminders of his predatory nature, his use of photography as a lure, and the countless lives he likely touched with his dark intentions. For families of the missing, these images offer a haunting glimmer of hope mixed with dread—the possibility of finding answers, but the terror of discovering the truth.

Alcala's legacy extends beyond the lives of his victims and their families. His story is a warning about the dangers of trusting appearances and a reminder of how easily a skilled manipulator can slip through the cracks. Alcala's ability to charm his way onto a national television show highlighted how dangerously deceptive outward appearances can be. He forces us to question our own assumptions about trust and safety, revealing the unsettling truth that sometimes, evil walks among us disguised as the most ordinary of faces.

Over time, Alcala has become both a symbol of justice delayed and a testament to the power of DNA technology in finally bringing closure. His case reveals flaws in the justice system while underscoring the triumph of forensic advancements, which eventually connected him to his crimes and prevented him from ever walking free. Alcala's story is a pivotal chapter in forensic science, showing how evidence can bring long-awaited answers to grieving families.

Yet for his victims' families, the knowledge of his conviction cannot undo the scars he left behind. Alcala's actions left lasting wounds that no courtroom verdict could heal. The loved ones of his victims continue to bear the weight of his crimes, holding on to the memories of those they lost and the knowledge that justice, though served, came far too late.

Rodney Alcala's story is a stark reminder of unchecked cruelty, the dangers of charisma, and the chilling reality of hidden malice. His legacy is one of horror, but it also speaks to the resilience of families who sought justice, investigators who doggedly pursued the truth, and a public determined never to forget his victims. It's a tale of darkness hidden behind charm and the reminder that, sometimes, the true face of evil is alarmingly ordinary.

Chapter Eight

The Convergence of Media and Violence

The complex relationship between media and violence has long fascinated and unsettled, especially when real-life horrors intersect with entertainment. Rodney Alcala's story is a chilling example of this uneasy balance. Known as *The Dating Game Killer*, Alcala's appearance on the lighthearted 1970s show highlights how media, often unknowingly, can serve as a platform for individuals who hide sinister intentions. Alcala charmed a national audience, winning a date with an unsuspecting bachelorette. But beneath his charismatic exterior was a man who had already committed horrific murders and would go on to claim more lives.

The case of Rodney Alcala underscores the disturbing truth that individuals capable of great harm can slip through the cracks, leveraging charm and the media to mask their dark intentions. His crimes force us to question the media's role in enabling dangerous personas. How could someone capable of such violence appear on a national TV show without raising any red flags? Alcala's presence on *The Dating Game* blurred the line between entertainment and real-life danger, becoming a haunting part of his legacy.

Since Alcala's time, true crime has exploded as a genre, captivating audiences with stories of crime, deception, and justice. Shows like *The Dating Game*, once purely a source of lighthearted fun, take on a sinister significance in retrospect. Alcala's participation on a dating show makes his story even more chilling, as it confronts viewers with the unsettling truth: a killer can appear perfectly ordinary. The entertainment industry's failure to recognize Alcala's danger highlights a broader issue: the media's tendency to prioritize spectacle over safety and substance.

Alcala's story also brings to light ethical questions surrounding media production. In shows like *The Dating Game*, casting choices were based on a contestant's personality and entertainment value rather than a thorough vetting of their background. As a result, a man with a dark history was granted a national stage simply because his crimes had not yet been fully exposed. This reliance on appearances created a dangerous oversight, allowing Alcala's charming demeanor to overshadow any scrutiny that could have prevented his participation.

In many ways, Alcala's media presence exemplifies the power of perception. He used his charm to craft a likable public persona, hiding his true nature behind a "charming bachelor" facade. This manipulation exposes a dangerous intersection where media and violence can coexist, with violent individuals using their appearances to secure public favor or evade suspicion. His ability to exploit his media image as a disguise emphasizes how easily predators can hide in plain sight.

The media's role in broadcasting Alcala's story has only grown since his crimes were first revealed, sparking a larger true crime movement in books, documentaries, and podcasts. While such stories often seek justice and awareness, there's a fine line between educating the public and sensationalizing violence. Alcala's case serves as a reminder of how quickly true crime content can turn exploitative, shifting focus from victims to perpetrators. In the early media coverage of Alcala's crimes, headlines like "The Dating Game Killer" drew readers in with the shocking contrast between his television persona and his true nature, transforming him into a kind of morbid celebrity while diminishing the stories of his victims.

Alcala's participation on *The Dating Game* is a haunting example of how media can inadvertently platform dangerous individuals. This dark twist illustrates the media's role in shaping public perception; had Alcala's crimes not come to light, his appearance might have remained a quirky footnote in television history. Instead, it became a symbol of the unsettling ways in which the media can be manipulated. Following his arrest, Alcala's case became a media sensation, with documentaries, books, and podcasts dissecting his life. His legacy thus serves as a case study of how media coverage can sometimes inadvertently perpetuate violence.

The convergence of media and violence isn't new, but Alcala's story brings it into sharp focus. His case compels us to confront the uncomfortable truth that, in its pursuit of ratings and sensational stories, the media can overlook the risks posed by individuals like Alcala. In an era dominated by reality TV and true crime fandom, Alcala's story serves as a sobering reminder of the responsibilities and ethical boundaries needed in media. It warns us of the dangers of accepting appearances at face value, and it challenges us to consider the real-world impact of the stories we consume so readily.

Printed in Great Britain
by Amazon